First published in the United States 1991 by

Atomium Books Inc.
Suite 300
1013 Centre Road
Wilmington, DE 19805

First edition published in French by Editions Fleurus, Paris, 1988,
under the title "Kouk et L'Ours de Glace."
Text and pictures copyright © Editions Fleurus 1988.
English translation and adaptation copyright © Atomium Books 1991.

Printed and bound in Belgium by
Color Print Graphix, Antwerp.
First U.S. Edition
ISBN 1-56182-029-6
2 4 6 8 10 9 7 5 3 1

Text: Ann Rocard   Illustrations: Morgan   English Adaptation: Linda Tyler

KOUK
AND THE ICE BEAR

atomium books

Kouk was a little Eskimo who loved to play and have fun.

One day Kouk's mom smiled at him and said, "Dad and I are going away for the day. Aunt Minnie and Uncle Buck have come to stay with you."

Kouk jumped up and down. "Oh boy! We can play all day!" he said.

Dad laughed. "Kouk, remember, Uncle Buck and Aunt Minnie have work to do. They can't play with you all the time!"

Then mom and dad hugged and kissed Kouk and waved good-bye.

Kouk wanted to play, but there was work to do. Aunt Minnie was busy in the kitchen. Uncle Buck was working on his carving.

Kouk's face spread into a big grin. He looked full of mischief.

"Minnie, can you find something for Kouk to do?" Uncle Buck called.

"Kouk, come help me wash the dishes," said Aunt Minnie.

Kouk was looking for fun, so he decided to wash the dishes in the snow.

"Buck!" shouted Aunt Minnie. "Please take this boy fishing so I can clean up the kitchen in peace!"

Uncle Buck was thinking about dinner and how many fish they would need. Kouk watched him cut a hole in the ice and drop his fishing line into the water. Uncle Buck watched and waited.

It seemed like a long time to Kouk. He started to get restless.

"A good fisherman must be patient," said Uncle Buck.

"Can we do something else?" asked Kouk.

"Be still or you'll scare the fish away," said Uncle Buck.

Kouk couldn't sit still. He was ready for some fun.

He tiptoed quietly behind Uncle Buck and gave him a big push into the fishing hole. "Now you have lots of fish, Uncle Buck," laughed Kouk.

Uncle Buck was so angry at Kouk that his face turned bright red.

He dragged Kouk to a nearby snowdrift. "Now just stay here where it's safe. You play by yourself while I finish fishing for our dinner tonight," he said.

Kouk sat in the snow and looked around. "If no one here has time to play with me, I'll have to find a friend who does," he decided.

Kouk took out his pocketknife and started chipping away at a block of ice. The ice block began to move under his feet. It was floating away from the snowdrift.

"Hooray," laughed Kouk. "I've made a ship. I'm going out to sea."

The ice block floated to the shore of an island. "This looks like fun," said Kouk.

He jumped onto the shore and started to run.

Suddenly, the icy ground below him split in two. Kouk's legs fell into the hole, so he stretched his arms to hold onto the edges.

Kouk looked down. The hole seemed to be getting deeper and deeper. His hands were slipping.

Kouk pulled himself up with all his might. Finally he was out of the big hole.

"Whew! That was a close call," he said out loud.

Kouk looked around and noticed some brightly colored balls on the
ice. "What are these?" he wondered.

He bent down and looked closely. "It looks like candy," he said.
He licked a green ball.

"Yum! Fruit-flavored ice candies." Kouk tasted each color.

"This is a great place!" he decided.

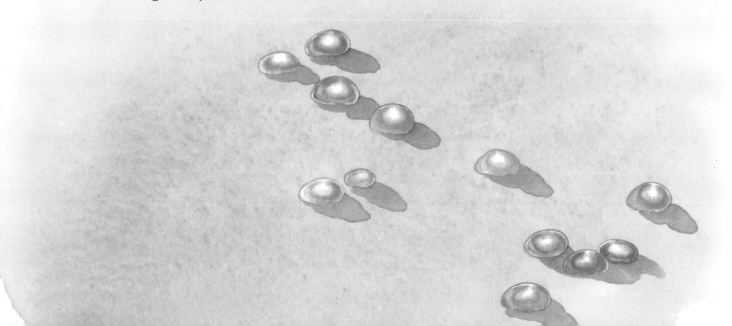

"Not for me," he heard a voice say.

Kouk turned around and saw a seal looking very sad.

"What's the matter?" Kouk asked.

"My ball is stuck in the ice and I can't get it out."

Kouk reached in his pocket and took out his pocketknife. He chipped away at the ice on each side of the ball. Suddenly the ball popped out into the air. The seal caught it on his nose.

"Thank you, little Eskimo, you're a good friend," said the grateful seal. He threw the big ball high into the air and started to do his favorite tricks. Kouk clapped his hands and laughed.

"Now it's your turn, little Eskimo," said the seal.

"Okay," said Kouk. He climbed up on the wheel. When he was ready, the seal threw the ball up onto Kouk's nose. Kouk tried to bounce it. Then he tried to do a back flip — and fell on his backside in the snow.

The seal barked with laughter.

"I think this trick is just for seals," said Kouk, feeling a little dizzy.

"But that was a good try," said the seal. "Thanks for helping me. If you ever need my help, just call out, 'I wish I were a seal.' I'll be there in a flash."

Kouk waved good-bye to his new friend and walked further along the island.

Soon Kouk heard voices singing. He ran to see who it could be.
"Hello, hello, hello," sang three oddly dressed penguins.
"Hi," said Kouk.
"Do you want to have some fun, fun, fun?" asked the penguins.
"Sure," said Kouk.
"Then follow us, us, us," they said.

The penguins started dancing and sliding on the ice.

"Come to our secret cave, cave, cave," the three penguins called.

"Okay," said Kouk. Off they went, sliding over the snowy hills, with Kouk riding on the shoulders of a penguin.

"I've never had so much fun in my whole life!" Kouk shouted with joy.

Kouk loved the giant icicles in the penguins' deep blue cave. The penguins told Kouk about the little ice elves who shared their cave and made toys from the icicles.

"I wish I could live here and play with all of you," said Kouk.

"Then stay, stay, stay," sang the penguins.

"No, my Uncle Buck will be finished fishing soon. I'd better get back home," said Kouk.

The penguins took Kouk back to
the hills.

"If you have any trouble getting back
home, just say 'I wish I were a penguin,
penguin, penguin,' and we will help you,
you, you," they all sang together.

"Thanks for all the fun," said Kouk. He
waved good-bye as he walked on.

Kouk sat down on the shore of the island. He felt very tired.

"Which way did I come from? Where's my ice block?" he said in a scared voice.

"What are you looking for?" asked a deep, mellow voice.

Kouk turned around and saw a big walrus with a wide smile on his face.

"Another friend!" thought Kouk to himself.

Kouk told the walrus about going out to sea on his ice block, and that his Uncle Buck would be waiting for him to come back. While he was talking, Kouk's stomach let out a loud rumble. He felt very hungry.

"Come to my cave for a snack before you go," said the friendly walrus.

"Okay, but just for a few minutes," Kouk said.

The big furry walrus gently took Kouk's hand as they walked to his cozy cave.

Kouk enjoyed the fresh fish the walrus gave him.

"Tell me about where you come from," said the walrus.

Kouk drew a map. He wrote the name of his village and his name. The walrus could not read.

"You're very smart, my little friend," said the walrus.

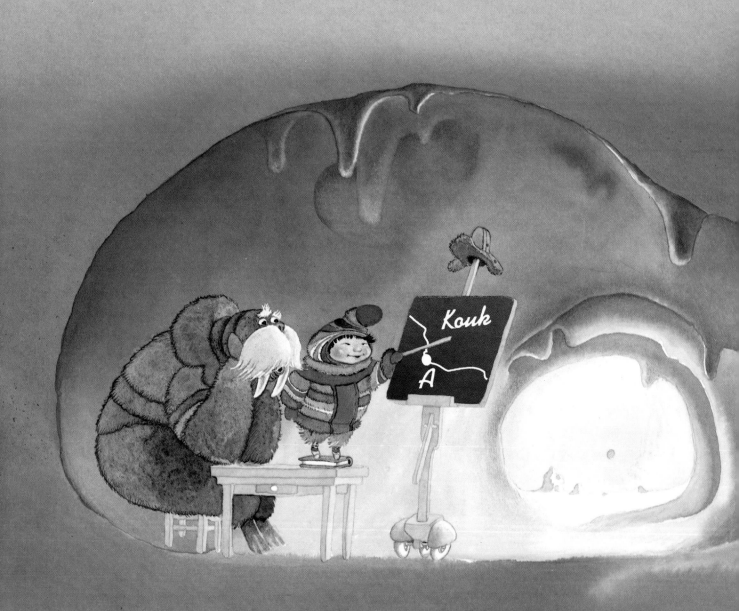

Kouk told the walrus about the tricks he had played on Aunt Minnie and Uncle Buck.

"Your family loves you very much," said the walrus. "They'll be worried about you. You must go back to them.

"Now go straight home and try your best to be good," the walrus told Kouk. "If you ever need me, just call out, 'I wish I were a walrus,' and I will come to help you."

Kouk started running toward the shore. "Thanks for everything," he called to the walrus, turning around for one last look. "That was so much fun."

Kouk still could not find his ice block so he decided to make a new one. While he was chipping at the ice he heard heavy footsteps crunching the deep snow behind him.

"Where do you think you are going, little Eskimo?"

Kouk heard the fierce tone in the voice. He was afraid to turn around.

"I'm going home to my Aunt Minnie and Uncle Buck," he said in a shaky voice. Looking up he saw a huge bear. Kouk shivered with fright.

"Why did you come here?" the bear asked.

"Because I wanted to have fun," Kouk said.

"Then come into my ice palace. I am the ice bear and I am very glad that you are here," said the giant white bear.

"Oh, no, I have to be going right now because Uncle Buck will be waiting for me. I've already stayed too long," Kouk said firmly.

The bear came closer. Kouk could see his icy claws coming toward him.

"It will only take a little time," the ice bear said sweetly.

"Okay, I'll come to your palace, but just for a few minutes. My Uncle Buck will really be worried about me," said Kouk.
He followed the bear to the ice palace.

The palace was a bright, shiny glass castle. The ice bear opened the door to a gigantic room filled with the most wonderful toys Kouk had ever seen.

"Enjoy yourself," said the ice bear.

Kouk didn't know which toy to try first. There were so many interesting things to play with.

The ice bear laughed with a mean tone in his voice as he watched Kouk fall into his trap.

"Little Eskimo, I want you to try my special food," said the ice bear.
Kouk found himself facing a table full of the most delicious desserts he had ever seen. He tasted them all and stuffed himself until he couldn't move.

"This is what we eat for every meal," laughed the ice bear.
Kouk was so full that he could hardly walk.

"Thank you," Kouk said to the ice bear. "Now I have to go home." Slowly he walked to the other end of the long hall. He turned around to say good-bye to the ice bear, but no one was there.

Kouk called out, "Ice bear." There was no answer.

At the end of the hall Kouk found a red curtain. He pulled it back. There in front of him was a huge ice maze.

"I'll never find my way out," Kouk sobbed. He felt scared. Tears began running down his face.

"How will I get back home?"

Kouk thought about all his friends and what they had told him to do if he was in trouble.

"I wish I were a seal," Kouk called out loudly.

Like magic, the seal's big ball appeared in front of Kouk.

"Follow the ball. It will lead you through the maze," he heard the seal's voice say.

Magically the ball rolled along, guiding Kouk to the back door of the ice palace.

The seal was waiting there. Kouk jumped into the seal's arms and hugged him.

"Hurry, hurry," said the seal. "Run as fast as you can!"

As Kouk was running he turned around and called out, "Thank you, seal. Thank you for saving me."

Behind him Kouk could hear the sound of the ice bear's feet.
"Grrr," growled the ice bear. "You're not going to get away from me!"
Kouk could feel his heart beating very fast. "Help!" yelled Kouk. He could feel the ice bear's cold breath on his back.
"My friends, I have more friends," thought Kouk. "I wish I were a penguin, penguin, penguin," he screamed.

In a flash Kouk found himself flying on a sled. The three penguins were pulling him down a hill at full speed. They stopped at the bottom, on the edge of the island. "Thank you, thank you," Kouk started to say.

"Quick, quick, quick," said the three penguins. "Call for more help! help! help!" The ice bear was running down the hill.

"I wish I were a walrus," Kouk shouted at the top of his lungs.

Before he even finished the last word, Kouk felt something furry under his feet.

Suddenly there was nothing but water all around Kouk.

"That was a close call, my little friend," said a deep, mellow voice.

Kouk looked down into the kind eyes of the walrus. His big furry friend was swimming him to safety.

Behind them the ice bear was in a rage. "I'll get you next time. You won't escape from me twice!" the ice bear growled.

The walrus took Kouk to the shore of his village.

"Good-bye. Be a good boy now," the walrus said as Kouk jumped onto the icy shore.

Kouk gave the walrus a big hug and kiss. "Good-bye. Thank you for saving me!"

By now everyone in the family was out looking for Kouk. Uncle Buck paddled up and down the shore watching for an ice block carrying Kouk. Aunt Minnie was looking in the snowdrifts, calling Kouk's name in her loudest voice. His mom and dad were looking in all the other houses in the village.

The sun had set. In the darkness Kouk followed the torch lights that
led from the shore to the village. Kouk felt so tired. His feet were
freezing cold from the wet trip home. The icy wind whipped his face.
"Mom, Dad, Aunt Minnie, Uncle Buck," he called out.
The village was just ahead, but to Kouk it still looked far away.

Kouk kept thinking about his family. Meeting the ice bear had taught him a lesson. Now he understood why he had to play where it was safe.

As Kouk saw his house ahead, he yelled, "I'm home! Hey, everyone, I'm home!"

Kouk's mom and dad ran out and scooped him up in their arms.

Uncle Buck and Aunt Minnie came running out to hug and kiss him.

"Uncle Buck, can we go fishing tomorrow? I'll sit with you and help you take the fish off your line," said Kouk.

"Yes, we can go fishing," laughed Uncle Buck. "But then I think we should play together in the snow and go for a long sled ride," he told Kouk.

Aunt Minnie stirred the fish stew as everyone listened to Kouk talk about his adventures.

"I will never stray away again," said Kouk.

He begged Aunt Minnie to let him help wash the dishes after dinner.

"I think we should all do the dishes together so we'll have time to play a game with you before you go to bed," she said.

"That's right, Kouk," said his mom and dad. "Let's all do the work together so we can all have time to play."